Little Narwhal's Day

A Secret Creatures Book

WRITTEN BY: ANGELA CASTILLO
ILLUSTRATIONS BY: INDIRA ZULETA

Copyright 2019, Angela Castillo
ISBN 978-1-95341908-8

Dedicated to all the children
who love sea creatures.

Little Narwhal's Day

A Secret Creatures Book

WRITTEN BY: ANGELA CASTILLO

ILLUSTRATIONS BY: INDIRA ZULETA

Little Narwhal wakes to
sunbeams streaming through
the cold Arctic waves.

"Good morning, my child,"
Mama Narwhal whistles.

Little Narwhal clicks,
"Good morning, Mama."

In a flurry of bubbles, Little Narwhal rises to the water's surface and bobs among chunks of ice.

A ribbon seal and
a puffin wave hello.

Two Arctic fox kits
tumble in the snow.

Little Beluga taps Little Narwhal's fin. "Wanna play?"

Little Narwhal chases Little
Beluga over the foaming waves.

A school of Arctic char swim by.
They are too busy to play.

The two friends play hide-and-swim
among the coral reefs.

After the fun game, Little Narwhal and Little Beluga float to the surface to breathe.

Arctic terns fly in lazy circles,
searching for lunch.

Northern lights flood the sky.
The two friends dive back into
the ocean depths.

Little Narwhal and Little Beluga
swim home on watercolor waves.

Fun facts about the
Arctic's Secret Creatures

► The horn of a narwhal is really a tusk, or tooth, much like an elephant's. They actually have two teeth, but most of the time only one grows into a tusk.

► Whistles and clicks are just two of the many sounds narwhals make. They use noises for echo location, to communicate, and just because.

► For a long time, scientists believed tusks were used to break through the ice or for defense, like a sword. But no one has seen narwhals do any of these things. Narwhals might use their tusk, which is very sensitive, to test the temperature of the water surrounding them.

► Ribbon seals can move across the ice as fast as a man can run for short distances.

► The beautiful white coat of an Arctic fox turns to a splotchy brown in the summer, after the snow melts, to help it blend into the dirt and rocks of the tundra.

► Beluga whales are the narwhal's closest cousins, and they have even been found sharing a family group, or pod together.

► The oldest Arctic char found was believed to be forty years old!

► Narwhals can stay underwater for up to 25 minutes. They breathe from blowholes on the tops of their heads.

► Northern lights can be many colors, including red, green, pink, blue and white.

Find out more!

About Narwhals:
https://dosits.org/galleries/audio-gallery/marine-mammals/toothed-whales/narwhal/

About the ribbon seal:
https://www.oceansoffun.org/pinniped_species/25
https://www.afsc.noaa.gov/nmml/education/pinnipeds/ribbon.php

About Arctic Foxes
https://www.nationalgeographic.com/animals/mammals/a/arctic-fox/

About Belugas
https://kids.nationalgeographic.com/animals/beluga-whale/#beluga-whale-underewater-closeup-teeth.jpg

Arctic Chars:
https://news.orvis.com/fly-fishing/fish-facts-arctic-char-salvelinus-alpinus

Coral Reefs:
http://wwf.panda.org/our_work/oceans/coasts/coral_reefs/coldwater_corals/

Northern Lights:
https://adventures.is/information/about-northern-lights/

Find out more about Angela Castillo and her books for kids at
http://tobythetrilby.weebly.com.
You can also find all her books, including novels for adults
and older kids, at Amazon.com for Kindle and paperback.

Coming soon, another
great picture book from
Angela Castillo.

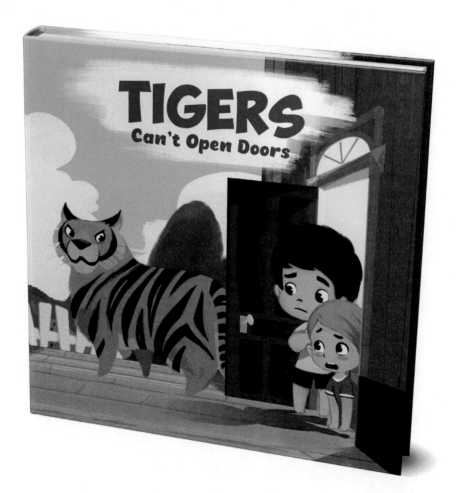

coming in Summer 2019